For Lori Nowicki

Henry Holt and Company
Publishers since 1866
175 Fifth Avenue, New York, New York 10010
mackids.com

Library of Congress Cataloging-in-Publication Data
Names: Slack, Michael H., 1969– author, illustrator.
Title: Turtle Tug to the rescue / Michael Slack.
Description: First Edition. | New York : Henry Holt and Company, 2017. |
Summary: "From panicking puffins to entangled sperm whales, Turtle Tug is
out to rescue all his sea-dwelling friends" —Provided by publisher.
Identifiers: LCCN 2016002102 | ISBN 9781627791946 (hardback)
Subjects: | CYAC: Stories in rhyme. | Turtles—Fiction. | Rescue work—Fiction. |
Marine animals—Fiction. | BISAC: JUVENILE FICTION / Animals / Turtles. |
JUVENILE FICTION / Transportation / Boats, Ships & Underwater Craft.
Classification: LCC PZ8.3.S6289 Tu 2017 | DDC [E]—dc23
LC record available at https://lccn.loc.gov/2016002102

Our books may be purchased in bulk for promotional, educational, or business use. Please contact
your local bookseller or the Macmillan Corporate and Premium Sales Department at (800) 221-7945
ext. 5442 or by e-mail at MacmillanSpecialMarkets@macmillan.com.

First Edition—2017 / Designed by April Ward
The illustrations for this book were digitally painted and collaged in Adobe Photoshop.
Printed in China by RR Donnelley Asia Printing Solutions Ltd., Dongguan City, Guangdong Province

1 3 5 7 9 10 8 6 4 2

TURTLE TUG
TO THE RESCUE

MICHAEL SLACK

Christy Ottaviano Books

Henry Holt and Company • New York

He cruises the coastline
with a keen, watchful eye,
guarding sea dwellers
swimming on by.

Serving the sea,
Tug chugs through
the day.

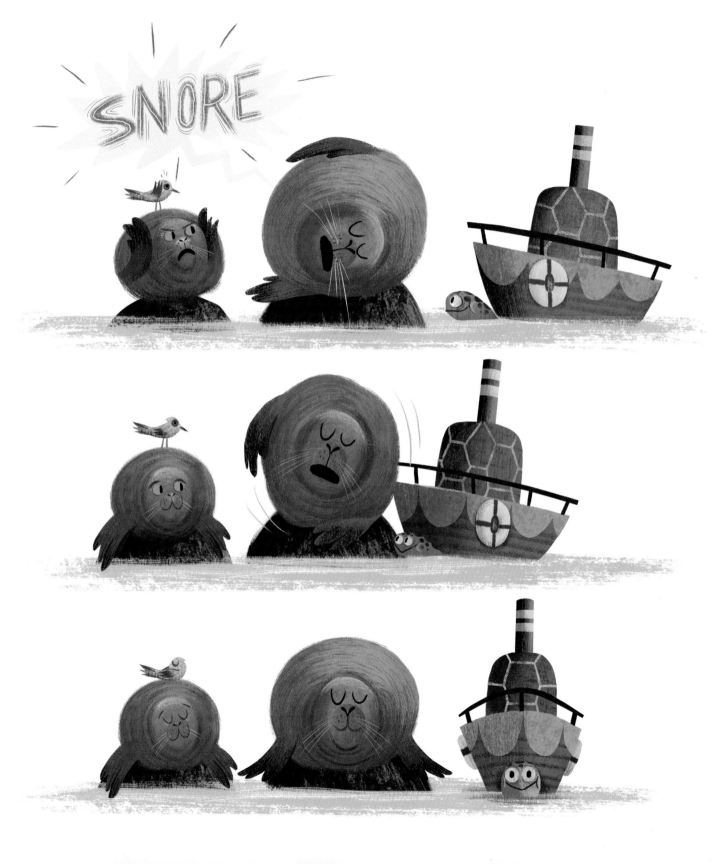

The skipper
with flippers is
leading the way.

The sun disappears.
Clouds gather
and form.

The ocean is brewing a
tempestuous
Storm.

Breezes become gusts.
The surge starts to grow.

The surf
isn't safe—

GO,
TURTLE TUG,
GO!

The tide turns
treacherous
as the rain
begins to **pour.**

Puffins are **panicking** drifting offshore.

A seal pup is **Stuck**.
Tug's there in a flash,

dodging sea cliffs
as breaking waves **crash.**

Whipping
winds
howl
as Tug
sails into a
gale,

dropping a **towline**

to an **entangled** sperm whale.

Charting his course,

Tug turns with a

CHUG!

GO, TURTLE TUG!

He weathers **rough waves,**
his bearings are set,
towing his **cargo** to
a harbored inlet.

A squid's in **trouble**
off Tug's starboard side.
It **latches** on tight and
hitches a **ride**.

What's that up ahead?
Shelter—
at last!

Tug keeps everyone **safe** till the **typhoon** has passed.

From stem to stern,
he's **loyal** as can be.
A special sea vessel,
steward of the **sea**.

TURTLE TUG!